A Lullaby of Love for

# Wren

By Suzanne Marshall

LiveWellMedia.com

ISBN-13: 978-1719364843
ISBN-10: 1719364842

This book is dedicated to

# WREN

who is loved very much!

# Wren,

are you ready to give thanks tonight

for all that is peaceful, warm and bright?

# Wren,

as the Deer plays guitar with glee,

we give thanks for you and me,

and our time together in harmony.

I AM
THANKFUL

# Wren,

as the Hippo plays the violin,

we give thanks for giggles and grins,

and belly laughs from deep within.

# Wren,

as the Owl drums like a pro,

we give thanks for adventures

that help us grow,

even "oopsy-daisies"

and "uh-ohs."

# Wren,

as the Giraffe softly sings,

we give thanks for everything,

like smooches from pooches,

and butterfly wings.

# Wren,

as the Eagle plays the harp,
we give thanks for your big heart;
you are brave and you are smart.

# Wren,

as the Badger plays clarinet,

we give thanks for every breath,

like each deep breath

that helps us rest.

# Wren,

as the Antelope plays maracas,

we give thanks for cuddles and hugs,

and all that is cozy,

comfy and snug.

# Wren,

as the Elk plays the cello,

we give thanks that you are mellow,

like a spongy, sweet marshmallow.

# Wren,

as the Bunny plays the violin,

we give thanks for family and friends,

and love that never,

ever ends.

# Wren,

as the Fox plays the flute,

I give thanks that you are YOU.

You are loved and loving too.

# Wren,

as the Bear plays the sax,

as you sleep, as you relax,

## I LOVE YOU

to the moon and back.

GOODNIGHT
WREN

# Credits

*Special thanks to my family and to my dear friends Hannah and Rachel Roeder. All illustrations have been edited by the author. Musical animals and hot-air balloon: © ddraw (freepik). Main cat, cat friend & sleeping kitty: © dazdraperma (fotosearch). Puppy: yayayoyo (fotosearch). Moon and lantern: © zzve (fotosearch). Floral ladder: © colematt (fotosearch). Additional elements were curated from freepik.*

## About the Author

An honors graduate of Smith College, Suzanne Marshall writes to inspire, engage and empower children. Learn more about Suzanne and her books at **LiveWellMedia.com**. *(Photo: Suzanne & Abby Underdog)*

# More Personalized Books from LiveWellMedia.com

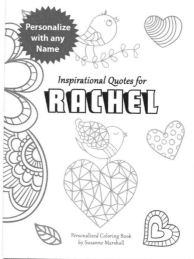

Made in the USA
Monee, IL
07 May 2022

96058195R00021